STEP-BY-STEP EXPERIMENTS WITH LIFE CYCLES

By Katie Marsico

Illustrated by Bob Ostrom

Published by The Child's World®
1980 Lookout Drive • Mankato, MN 56003-1705
800-599-READ • www.childsworld.com

ACKNOWLEDGMENTS
The Child's World®: Mary Berendes, Publishing Director
The Design Lab: Design and production
Red Line Editorial: Editorial direction
Consultant: Diane Bollen, Project Coordinator, Mars Rover Mission,
    Cornell University

ISBN 9781609735876
LCCN 2011940142

PHOTO CREDITS
Karel Gallas/Dreamstime, cover; Pilar Echeverria/Dreamstime, cover,
back cover; Tsombos Alexis/Dreamstime, 1, 29; Anke Van Wyk/Dream-
stime, 4; Artography/Shutterstock Images, 8, 31; Mau Horng/Shut-
terstock Images, 12; Adrian Matthiassen/Dreamstime, 17; Dirk Ercken/
Shutterstock Images, 18; Kerstin Klaassen/iStockphoto, 21; Shutterstock
Images, 25; Amy Johansson/Shutterstock Images, 27; Gabi Moisa/
Dreamstime, 28

Design elements: Pilar Echeverria/Dreamstime, Robisklp/Dreamstime,
Jeffrey Van Daele/Dreamstime, Sarit Saliman/Dreamstime

Printed in the United States of America

BE SAFE !

The experiments in this book are
meant for kids to do themselves.
Sometimes an adult's help is
needed though. Look in the
supply list for each experiment.
It will list if an adult is needed.
Also, some supplies will need to
be bought by an adult.

TABLE OF CONTENTS

4

Baby and adult elephants are in different parts of their life cycles.

CHAPTER ONE

Study Life Cycles!

Have you changed at all since you were born? Of course you have! So do other living things. Plants and animals have life cycles. A life cycle is made up of all the changes that happen as living things grow.

Many plants and animals have simple life cycles. Their lives are made up of three main stages. The first is the time before they are born. The second is the time when they are young. And the third is the time when they are adults. Some animals go through a few other stages during their life cycles. How can you learn more about life cycles?

CHAPTER TWO

Seven Science Steps

Doing a science **experiment** is a fun way to discover new facts.
An experiment follows steps to find answers to science questions.
This book has experiments to help you learn about life cycles.
You will follow the same seven steps in each experiment:

Seven Steps

1. Research: Figure out the facts before you get started.

2. Question: What do you want to learn?

3. Guess: Make a **prediction**. What do you think will happen in the experiment?

4. Gather: Find the supplies you need for your experiment.

5. Experiment: Follow the directions.

6. Review: Look at the results of the experiment.

7. Conclusion: The experiment is done. Now it is time to reach a **conclusion**. Was your prediction right?

Are you ready to become a scientist? Let's experiment to learn about life cycles!

CHAPTER THREE

What's Best for the Bean?

What do you know about a plant's life cycle? Find out if plants need certain things to change and grow.

Research the Facts

Here are a few facts. What else can you learn?

- A plant begins its life cycle as a seed.
- A plant ends its life cycle after it creates and releases new seeds.

Ask Questions

- Does light change a plant's life cycle?
- Does water help plants grow?

A plant grows from a pinto bean.

Make a Prediction

Here are two examples:

- Light and water change how a plant grows.
- Light and water will not change how a plant grows.

Gather Your Supplies!

- 2 clear plastic cups
- A permanent marker
- 2 dried pinto beans
- 1/2 cup of water
- 2 cups of potting soil
- Pencil or pen
- Paper
- A camera (optional)

Time to Experiment!

1. Use the marker to label one cup. On one cup, write: #1. Label the other cup: #2.

2. Fill each cup with some potting soil.

3. Plant the beans along the sides of the cups. This way you can see them through the plastic.

4. Cover the beans with more potting soil.

5. Put cup #1 in a sunny area. A counter or window are good spots. Place cup #2 in a dark spot in the same room.

6. Water cup #1 every day for the next two days. Do not water cup #2.

7. Study your beans at the end of two days. Is one bean plant growing better than the other? Does one plant look greener? Write down what you notice. Be sure to draw pictures or take photos.

Review the Results

Read your experiment notes. Study your photos and pictures. Did the bean plant in cup #1 grow well? How about the bean plant in cup #2? The bean plant that got water and sunlight grew better.

What Is Your Conclusion?

Did you predict the right answer? Sunlight and water make plants grow. They become green and healthy. A plant that is not in the sunlight is whiter. Plants use sunlight to make **chlorophyll**. This makes them green.

Water makes seeds sprout. This is when they begin growing into a plant.

The first part of an insect's life cycle is in its egg.

12

CHAPTER FOUR

What Comes after the Worm?

How do some insects grow? Some go through big changes during their life cycles. In this experiment, you will watch wax worms grow. They are a type of caterpillar.

Research the Facts

Here are a few. What else do you know?

- Most insects change several times during their life cycles. Insects often change form as they grow. This is called **metamorphosis**.
- An insect hatches from an egg. It is called a **larva**.
- An insect later changes into a **pupa**. It is closer to becoming an adult.
- The last stage of an insect's life is adulthood.

13

Ask Questions

- Do insects look different after metamorphosis?
- What ways do they change?

Make a Prediction

Here are two examples:

- Insects look different as they grow.
- Insects look the same their entire life cycle.

14

Gather Your Supplies!

- Adult help
- A container of wax worms (found at pet stores or bait shops)
- A large glass jar with lid
- Nail
- 1 cup uncooked oatmeal
- 1/4 cup sugar
- 1/4 cup hot water
- A paper bag
- Pencil or pen
- Paper
- A camera (optional)

Time to Experiment!

1. Have an adult do this step. Poke holes in the lid of the jar with a nail. This allows the wax worms air to breathe.

2. Place oatmeal into the jar. Mix the sugar and water. Add it to the jar, too.

3. Gently drop your wax worms into the jar. Tightly screw on the lid.

4. How do the wax worms look now? Record what you see. You can also draw pictures or take photos.

5. Put the jar in a paper bag. Place the bag in a warm spot in your house.

6. Remove the jar from the bag every few days. Write down how the wax worms look each time. Are they changing at all? Remember to draw pictures or take photos.

7. At the end of six weeks, bring your jar outside. Let your wax worms go. They may not look like worms anymore, though!

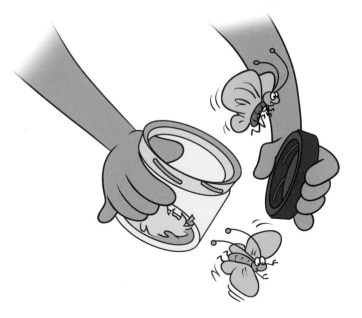

Review the Results

Study your notes. Look at your pictures and photos. How did the wax worms change? Did they get bigger? Did they change color or shape? The wax worms should have changed in shape and color.

What Is Your Conclusion?

What did you learn? Wax worms start out with soft, white bodies. During the last part of their life cycle, they become moths! These changes are part of their metamorphosis.

Wax worms build cocoons. Inside the cocoons they change into moths.

18

Tree frogs spend much of their lives in trees.

CHAPTER FIVE

Who Makes a Move?

Some animals move from water to land as they grow. They change as they grow. What changes do their bodies make? Try this to see what happens to a frog's body as it grows.

Research the Facts

Here are a few facts. What else can you find?

- A few animals live in water during the early parts of their life cycle.
- Some animals move onto land as their bodies change and grow.
- Frogs are called tadpoles during the early parts of their life cycle.

Ask Questions

- What kinds of animals live on land and in water?
- How does an animal's body change as it moves from land to water?

Make a Prediction

Here are two examples:

- Frogs' and tadpoles' bodies are different.
- Frogs' and tadpoles' bodies are the same.

- Pencil or pen
- Paper
- A camera (optional)

Time to Experiment !

1. Find the best place to watch tadpoles for 15 to 30 minutes. Ponds or streams are both good spots. You can also find tadpoles at aquariums, pet stores, and fish-supply stores.

Tadpoles live in the water.

2. Watch the tadpoles. How do they look? Do they always stay in the water? Do they ever spend time on land? Write down everything you see. You should also draw pictures or take photos.

3. Now find the best place to watch adult frogs for 15 to 30 minutes. You might spot some near ponds and streams. A lot of pet stores and aquariums also sell them.

4. Study the adult frogs. How do they look? Are they in the water? Do they spend any time on land? Write what you see. Remember to draw pictures or take photos.

Review the Results

Study your notes. Look at your photos and pictures. How do tadpoles and frogs look different? How do tadpoles and frogs live differently? Tadpoles have no legs and stay in the water all the time. Frogs have legs and spend some time on land.

What Is Your Conclusion?

What did you learn? You've seen that tadpoles change to become adult frogs. Legs allow frogs to move on land. Tadpoles can only breathe in the water. Frogs breathe air.

Newts, salamanders, and toads have the same life cycle as a frog. They begin life in the water but end up living on land.

CHAPTER SIX

Seed Search

Seeds are made at the end of a plant's life cycle. Where are seeds found? Find out in this tasty test!

Research the Facts

Here are a few. What else do you know?

- Plants produce seeds.
- Inside each seed is the material to make a new plant.

Ask Questions

- Are seeds found in fruits?
- Are seeds found in vegetables?

Make a Prediction

Here are two examples:

- You can find seeds in fruits and vegetables.
- You will not find seeds in fruits and vegetables.

Many flowers' seeds grow from the head of the flower.

Gather Your Supplies!

- An adult
- A knife
- An apple
- A green pepper
- Pencil or pen
- Paper

Time to Experiment!

1. Wash your apple and green pepper.
2. Ask an adult to slice the apple down the middle.

3. Do you see any seeds inside the fruit? Write down everything you see.
4. Now ask the adult to slice a green pepper in half. Do you see any seeds inside this vegetable? Be sure to record what you notice.
5. When you are finished, you can snack on the apple and green pepper. Put the leftovers back in the refrigerator.

What is inside a green pepper?

Review the Results!

Look over your notes. Review your drawings. Did you find seeds inside the apple and the green pepper? The apple and green pepper both had seeds inside.

What Is Your Conclusion?

Was your prediction right? Vegetables and fruits do have seeds. Some plants make fruits and vegetables that contain seeds. This happens near the end of a plant's life cycle.

Plant seeds come in many different shapes and sizes. Some are as large as coconuts! Coconuts are the seeds of the coconut tree.

You are a scientist now. What fun life cycle facts did you learn? You found out that plants need sunlight and water to grow. You saw that caterpillars and frogs change form as they grow. You can learn even more about life cycles. Study them. Experiment with them. Then share what you learn about life cycles.

Glossary

chlorophyll (klor-uh-fil): Chlorophyll is green matter in plants that uses the sun's energy to make food. Green plants have chlorophyll.

cocoons (kuh-KOONS): Cocoons are silky cases that some animals create for their bodies or eggs. Insects change inside cocoons.

conclusion (kuhn-KLOO- shuhn): A conclusion is what you learn from doing an experiment. The conclusion was that different fruits make seeds.

experiment (ek-SPER-uh-ment): An experiment is a test or way to study something to learn facts. The class did an experiment using plants.

larva (LAR-vuh): A larva is an animal soon after hatching that looks very different from its parents. An insect changes from a larva to a pupa.

metamorphosis (met-uh-MOR-fuh-siss): Metamorphosis is the series of changes some animals go through between hatching and adulthood. Caterpillars go through a metamorphosis.

prediction (pri-DIKT-shun): A prediction is what you think will happen in the future. One prediction is that seeds grow in flowers.

pupa (PYOO-puh): A pupa is an insect in the life cycle stage between larva and adult. An insect changes from a pupa to an adult.

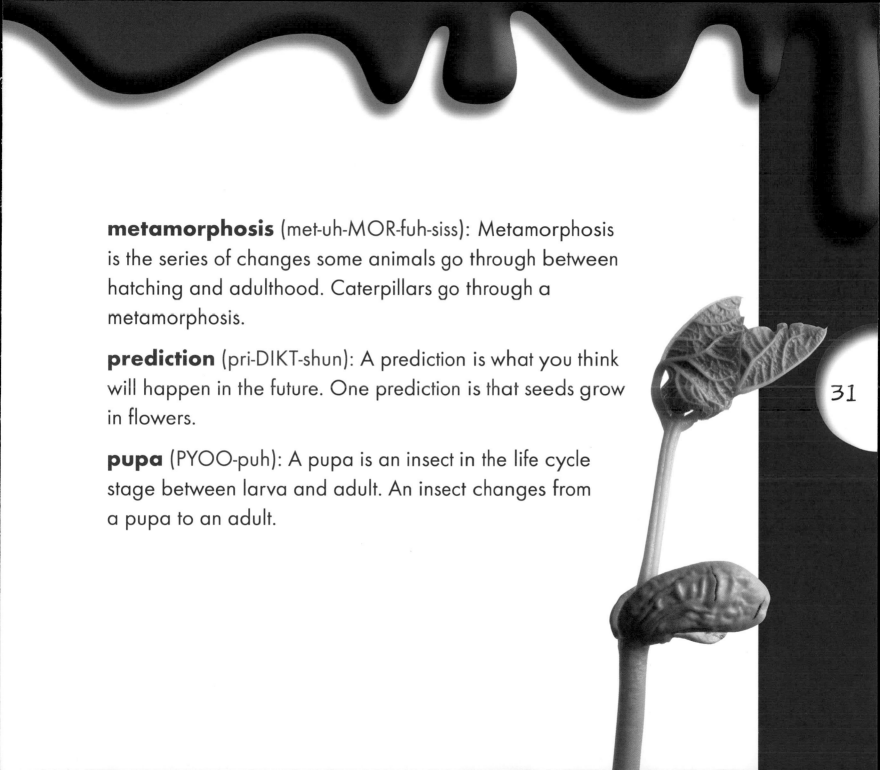

Books

De la Bédoyère, Camilla. *Tadpole to Frog*. Irvine, MN: QEB Publishing, 2009.

Reilly, Kathleen M. *Explore Life Cycles! 25 Great Projects, Experiments, Activities*. White River Junction, VT: Nomad Press, 2011.

Solway, Andrew. *Secrets of Animal Life Cycles*. New York: Marshall Cavendish Benchmark, 2010.

Index

32

Web Sites

Visit our Web site for links about life cycle experiments:
childsworld.com/links

Note to Parents, Teachers, and Librarians: We routinely verify our Web links to make sure they are safe and active sites. So encourage your readers to check them out!

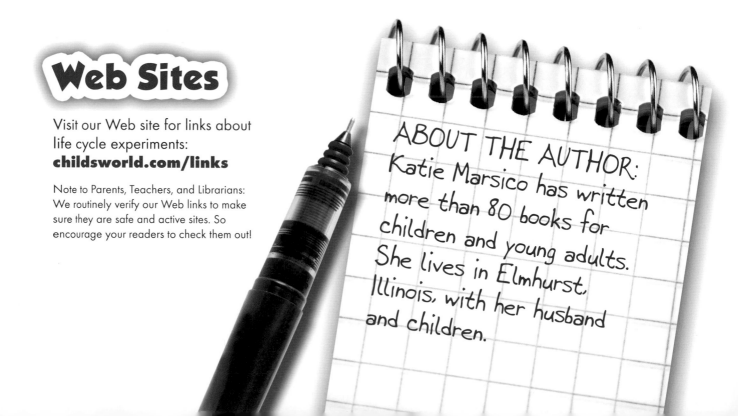

ABOUT THE AUTHOR: Katie Marsico has written more than 80 books for children and young adults. She lives in Elmhurst, Illinois, with her husband and children.